Apprentice Witches

by

Roger J. Burnett

Gotham Books

30 N Gould St.
Ste. 20820, Sheridan, WY 82801
https://gothambooksinc.com/

Phone: 1 (307) 464-7800

© 2024 *Roger J. Burnett*. All rights reserved.

No part of this book may be reproduced, stored in a retrieval system, or transmitted by any means without the written permission of the author.

Published by Gotham Books (May 14, 2024)

ISBN: 979-8-88775-914-2 (P)
ISBN: 979-8-88775-915-9 (E)

Because of the dynamic nature of the Internet, any web addresses or links contained in this book may have changed since publication and may no longer be valid.

The views expressed in this work are solely those of the author and do not necessarily reflect the views of the publisher, and the publisher hereby disclaims any responsibility for them.

Contents

Chapter 1 1

Chapter 2 19

Chapter 3 32

Chapter 4 39

Chapter 5 44

Chapter 6 51

Chapter 7 54

Chapter 8 63

Chapter 9 70

Chapter 10 75

Chapter 11 78

Chapter 12 81

Chapter 1

This month's cover of "Rock Fan" magazine splashed the figures and grotesquely painted faces of the world's latest rock band rage "Lucifer's Lockets". Their smashing new hit song, "Give Me a Minute of Your Time", was "Taking the Country by Storm", the headline screamed.

Isabel sat in bed with her back resting against a pillow reading the details of the group's mysterious explosion into stardom. They chose not to reveal their background and were never seen without their gnarled painted faces used to obscure their identity.

Her eyes blurred for a second and snapped open when the magazine slapped her on the chin as it dropped to her chest. Ten o'clock, time for lights out.

Her green and white plaid flannel pajamas looked nice with her red hair. Her mom often told her so. From Isabel's point of view, warm and comfy was enough since she wasn't trying to make a fashion statement in her pajamas.

Not only were her jammies old, but the legs were also at the high-water level well above her ankles. She obviously had grown some. This reminded her of her doctor's office visit a week ago. To her credit, she had an athletic body at a hundred and twenty pounds and five foot four. This was in the acceptable percentile for sixteen-year-olds.

She turned the bedside light off, punched her pillow to make a hollow for her head, and snuggled deep into the dent she made.

A moment later her eyes snapped open, bulging out of their sockets as they tried to see in the darkness. The green numbers on the bedside clock glared at midnight. What, I just closed my eyes a moment ago and it was only ten o'clock, she thought.

Waking up in the middle of the night is unusual for her. She usually sleeps like a log all night: unless she drinks a lot of water before bed.

She didn't have to go potty. But something woke her: Perhaps a barking dog or a catfight somewhere outside?

She lay still and listened for any sound. Her eyes moved from one side to the other in quick succession.

A cloudy sky and no moonlight to lessen the blackness of her room increased her anxiety.

To make things worse, she sensed a menacing presence in her room and starring at her.

At sixteen years old, the idea of a boogieman or ghost didn't seem like an option. It's not an option with the lights on. Now in the pitch-blackness of her bedroom, a ghost was a real possibility.

Goosebumps on her arms multiplied over her entire body. She pinched her cheek hard to confirm she wasn't dreaming. It hurt and confirmed she was at least awake. She bolted upright in bed.

"Who's there?" she murmured. She didn't want to yell and wake the rest of the house. Her parents would come rushing into her room to find out she was dreaming. How embarrassing.

"Who's there," she asked.

A woman's voice said, "Grandma Wilma and Miss Daisy Dobbins".

A dark figure moved from her bedroom door towards her. She shuffled backwards in bed pushing hard against the headboard.

She couldn't make out the face, but the voice sounded familiar.

"Is that you Grandma? Who is Miss Daisy?"

"One question at a time dear," the voice said, "Turn on your bedside light. We need to talk."

The lamp brightened by itself. Isabel hadn't touched the switch. Too weird she thought. Her head snapped back in the direction of the voice.

A tall slender woman, taller than Grandma but about the same age stood staring at her. The person's dark eyes twinkled as they adjusted to the light. She wore an all-black dress covering her from neck to toe. A pale face, with a wart on a pointy nose all seemed to remind her of the wicked witch from a book she had once read.

"You're not my grandmother. Where is she?"

"Stop asking two questions each time you open your mouth. No, I'm not your grandmother. I'm Miss Daisy."

"No, she's not but I am," her grandmother's voice said. She moved from behind Miss Daisy where Isabel could see her.

"What are you doing here? Why are you dressed in black?"

"Because," she said.

The image moved closer. With the help of the light that "she" didn't turn on, she could just make out a black outline topped with a tall, peaked hat and the tip bent over pointing to her left. On the band above the brim the word "front", was printed in white letters and glowed in the dim light.

"Why are you dressed like that? Were you at a Halloween party?"

"Because, and No! Please stop asking two questions at a time."

"Then you stop with the 'because'? You're making me crazy. Why are you dressed like a witch?"

"Because. . . I am a Witch."

"Really? Her grandmother's friend is a wicked witch?" Boo hoo, scary, scary. She waved her hands in the air like a white-sheeted ghost fluttering in the breeze. "I don't believe you."

"Be careful what you say young lady, or I'll turn you into a toad, too."

Her Grandmother came out from behind Miss Daisy's shadow. She wore the same witch's costume.

They walked in single file, which allowed enough room to pass through her bedroom door. Isabel always keeps the door locked to discourage her two younger brothers from entering unannounced. A locked door didn't seem to bother Grandma and Ms. Daisy.

"No more toad incantations," Grandma said to Miss Daisy. "We're in enough trouble."

"A toad?" What are you talking about," Isabel asked?

Miss Daisy raised her arm and tossed a big black sack on Isabel's bed close to where she was sitting. The bag twitched and wiggled. Isabel envisioned a bag of snakes.

Isabel's mouth opened to scream but no sound came out. Her vocal cords locked up.

"Don't even think about screaming. I've temporarily frozen your vocal cords so you can only speak in a whisper," Miss Daisy said.

Isabel jumped out of bed holding her throat with both hands and at the same time surveying the package on her bed.

"Open it", Miss Daisy said.

A drawstring weaved through the hem of the bag and a slipknot kept the top scrunched closed. In terror-based trepidation, Isabel forced her fingers to gingerly untie the knot and loosen the drawstring by grabbing the bag at the outside top. With the tips of her fingers, she turned the bag upside down and dumped the contents on the bed. At the same time, she bounced backward away from the now empty bag.

To her surprise, two large green bullfrogs tumbled out of the bag and landed on her bed.

She tried to scream but lost her voice again.

"Is this what I think it is?" She said when she regained control of herself, and her voice came back. "No... that is 'who' you think they are. "Miss Daisy said.

"Don't worry honey. It's just Josh and Ethan." Grandma said.

"Josh and Ethan? Why would you do that? Grandmothers don't turn their grandchildren into 'bullfrogs'!"

"I do," Miss Daisy said.

"But that was a mistake", Grandma corrected.

Isabel looked in the direction of the bed to confirm what she thought she was seeing. Two large green bullfrogs, each the size of a softball, sat on her bed.

"I thought you said toads."

"Frogs toads, toads' frogs, maybe I got them mixed up a little. Toads are ugly enough. All I wanted to do was to make a point. Frogs are equally as bad don't you think?"

Isabel looked closer at the bullfrogs. Their faces were human while their bodies were that of a frog.

There was no mistaking who the faces were. Their freckles gave them away. Freckles were a family trait. All Burnetts are born with carrot-red hair and freckles.

Josh and Ethan's mouths moved. However, the sound was faint. Miss Daisy had quieted them down as she had done to Isabel.

Get us out of here," Ethan yelled in a whisper. He was very scared. Josh looked around Isabel's room for his baseball bat that he keeps by his bed for protection.

Tears spilled down Isabel's cheeks. No matter what they did, they didn't deserve this she thought.

Fear now crept into her body as reality washed over her. Her mouth hung open.

"Why did you turn my brothers into bullfrogs?"
"Am I next?" Isabel was becoming angry.

Her grandmother said, "One question at a time dear. It confuses Miss Daisy. To answer your first question, yes, that is Joshua, and the other is Ethan."

"My Mom and Dad are going to have a hairball when they find out about this."

"Perhaps they'll never remember. Or. . . perhaps I'll turn you and your parents into toads", Miss Daisy threatened.

Isabel didn't try to correct her about the difference between frogs and toads but said, "You wouldn't dare."

"Oh, wouldn't I."

She raised her arm holding a knotty branch from a small bush. The tip twinkled.

"W... w... w... wait... wait," Grandma said in a panicky tone. "She believes you, Miss Daisy."

"Okay then, a little more respect for us elders are required around here if you ask me."

"Why are you doing this? Don't you love us anymore, Grandma?" Tears continued to stream down Isabel's face as her brothers wiggled around the bed and in full knowledge, they had no way to change their predicament.

"There you go again two questions. One at a time please."

"Of course, I love you dear."

"Then why did you turn Josh and Ethan into bullfrogs?"

"I didn't. It is all a mistake. Miss Daisy and I attended our meeting of the Sovereign Sisterhood of Good Witches where full regalia including pointy hats are required. On the way home I decided to come over to visit you and your brothers and to make sure you had nice dreams. I do every night, you know. Miss Daisy decided to come along with me."

"And?" Isabel nodded her head to suggest Grandma should continue.

"You are so pretty when you're asleep." Grandma smiled at the memory and touched her cheek with her right index finger. "I tripped over something on Josh's bedroom floor and the noise woke him. Ethan heard the noise and he ran into Josh's room. "

"I tried to tell them it was me," Grandma said. "They didn't believe me. Josh was so scared he grabbed his baseball bat to protect himself. Ethan threw his baseball glove at Miss Daisy trying to distract her while Josh bonked her with his bat."

"He knocked my 'Yo-mum,' off and bent the tip", Miss Daisy said and pointed to her black hat.

"Yo-mum?"

"Yo-mum is an ancient word for our pointed hat. We call it a 'Pointy" now. Anyway, Miss Daisy said her hocus-pocus words "under her breath and turned the boys into toads before I could react."

"Bullfrogs?"

"Okay, bullfrogs . . . anyway. . . I need to figure out a way to reverse the incantation. In the melee, Miss Daisy forgot the words of her witch's palindrome."

"Forgot the words? What kind of a witch forgets the words to an incantation?"

"An old one", Ms. Daisy piped in.

"How can I help?" I don't know any incantations, I'm not even sure I believe this whole thing is happening. Am I having a dream?" Her cheek still hurt where she had pinched herself earlier and that answered her question.

"Two questions", Grandma said and waved her finger at Isabel.

"This is no dream and no joke," Miss Daisy said.

Isabel went to sit on the edge of her bed.

"Don't sit on your brothers dear," Grandma said.

She jumped up visualizing the idea of sitting on her brothers and squashing them flat. She moved them over and sat down.

"Okay, say this is all for real. What do you want me to do?"

"Thank you, dear. Witches use an immediate reaction word to protect them from danger. This gives us time to think of and say the right words that are more appropriate to ward off the danger. "The words are like 'Palindromes'."

"What is a Pal-in-drome? I never heard that word before," she said.

"Palindromes are words that are spelled the same way forwards and in reverse. For example, like 'MOM or DAD", Grandma explained. "We use our special palindrome, which is a word spelled one way and a new word when spelled in reverse. For example, the word 'saw' becomes 'was' when spelled backward."

"I get it."

"All we do is say the word, touch our Ankh, and point our twinkle stick or my first finger at the danger. Presto, the danger is gone and reappears as whatever we were thinking about when we said the word."

"How did Josh and Ethan become bullfrogs?"

"Kind of complicated," Grandma said.

"If you expect me to help, I should know what happened."

"You are right. It would be better if Ms. Daisy explained.

"My palindrome is the word 'WARTS'. To reverse the spell, I use the word 'STRAW'. The problem is when

I said the word WARTS, I wondered why toads have warts and frogs don't. Next thing you know, zap, your brothers, became two bullfrogs. I can't find a palindrome with the words, 'Two Frogs,'" she said and shook her head in sadness.

Isabel glanced at her side where Josh and Ethan had moved closer to her. She wasn't fond of frogs, all slimy and such. But those were her brothers. Their eyes were tear-filled and revealed their fear. They understood the problem and didn't like what was being said as a solution.

"Now, let's stay calm," Grandma said. She saw the fear in Isabel's brother's eyes. "We've still got time."

"What do you mean we have time? Are we on a timetable or a clock?"

"There you go again. One question at a time dear."

"This is getting scary. Do you mean we are on the clock, a time limit?"

"Yes," Miss Daisy said.

"How much time?"

"We are given one minute for each letter in the palindrome word we use."

Isabel counted the letters of the word "warts" on her fingers.

"Five? You mean only five minutes?"

"No, about three minutes more or less. We've spent some time trying to reverse the spell before we woke you."

"Three minutes!"

"Don't panic. We have lots of time to find the reverse spell," Grandma said.

"Wrong. . . Isabel said. She too was now panicking. Three minutes is not long at all."

She couldn't understand the words Josh and Ethan yelled, but they were panicking along with her after hearing what Grandma just said. She was sure she heard Josh yell, "Get us out of here!" His face was flushed red, and Ethan's was, too. Both nodded their heads rapidly as confirmation.

"How do you reverse the spell," Isabel asked trying to calm herself. Rational thinking was the only way to help.

"You say the palindrome word in reverse and point your finger. Presto, the spell is reversed."

"Okay, let's try it. 'Straw!' Miss Daisy said and pointed her wand at Josh and Ethan. The two bullfrogs remained on Isabel's bed looking back at her but now not moving.

"See what we mean. Nothing works, Grandma said. "Time's running out. If we don't reverse the spell before the time expires, they'll stay like that for five hours, then five days, then five months, and then five years. It only gets worse. "

Having to make accurate decisions under stress was not Isabel's strong suit. This was the exception.

"Okay, let's settle down. We need to concentrate for a second."

Isabel's mind was racing, and she tried to control her emotions.

"Let's write all the words you said on a piece of paper. Say the words exactly as you did before." Isabel suggested.

"That sounds like an excellent idea," Grandma said. She handed her a piece of paper and a pencil.

"Where did that come from?" She really didn't want to hear the answer.

"Okay... number-one, you said 'Warts,' correct?"

"Correct."

"Two, you pointed your wand at Josh and Ethan, right?"

"Right."

"Next you thought of toads, and then frogs right?"

"Right."

"Then presto they were frogs, right?

"Right. What an intelligent child you are."

"Okay let's do it in reverse," Isabel suggested.

"First say 'STRAW' and then point your wand at the frogs and think of Josh and Ethan. Please hurry we don't have much time left."

"STRAW," Miss Daisy said. She pointed her pointy stick at the bullfrogs and grabbed the necklace hanging from her neck. She closed her eyes and mumbled something.

Isabel hoped she was thinking about her brothers and not something else. Grandma had her eyes closed tight. Her fingers crossed as well. Isabel closed her eyes.

The bed giggled. Isabel's eyes flashed open. The room had darkened and became silent. Her light was now off so she turned it back on and ran to Josh's room.

The soft blue lights of his aquarium and the sound of bubbling water filled the room as usual. He was sleeping soundly with his baseball bat resting by his right hand. Ethan's baseball glove lay on the floor by the door. That was unusual as Ethan was the most organized kid she knew. He always keeps his stuff in his room neatly packed away. She dashed across the hall to Ethan's room and he too lay fast asleep.

Isabel's Dad opened his bedroom door, wakened by the noises she made.

"What's going on?" He said. Her mother came and stood beside him.

"I was going to the bathroom."

"Are you planning on going to the bathroom in the hall," her mother asked.

"Of course not," Isabel said embarrassed by the conversation. "I thought I heard a noise."

Her Dad gave one of his patented eyebrow raises he used to mean he was confused.

"See you in the morning. Sorry for waking you." Isabel walked back to her room and listened for her parents' bedroom door to close.

As she walked across the bedroom, her foot touched something on the floor. She didn't jump because something always hung on the floor in her room. Not taking any chances of what could be on the floor, she glanced down and saw a pointy witch's hat. She picked it up and inspected the tip. It flopped to the left. The word "front" printed in white across the band, shone in the dim room.

"Miss Daisy wants you to have her old hat," Grandma said.

Isabel jumped in surprise.

"I thought you'd left."

"We couldn't go until we apologized."

"Right. I'm so sorry for all the fuss. I decided to retire from the "Sovereign Sisterhood of Good Witches" and turn in my twinkle stick. "

"You don't have to do that. Everything turned out fine."

"Oh, but I do dear. It's time for me to retire."

"I'm sorry to hear that but I know you'll make the right decision."

"There's still something else you need to know," Grandma said.

"And what would that be?"

"It's a long story."

"I want to hear it."

"Okay then. . . When a baby is born to our family, the 'Sovereign Sisterhood of Good Witches, the grandmother's branch' passes on to the new baby not one, but two palindromes to use when they need help. One is the word 'Mom' and the other is the word 'Dad'. Say the word and see them in your mind's eye and they will always be there to help you.

"What happens if they're not near when I need help?"

"They are always there in spirit even when you can't see them. All you do is close your eyes, say the palindrome, and visualize your parents. They will always be there to guide you."

"Do you mean I can ask for anything I want and get it?"

"No, it's not that kind of help. Should you need another opinion to decide, they will give you their point of view. Sometimes it will not be what you want to hear."

"I understand."

"Well, it's time we let you go back to sleep. When you wake up in the morning, you will remember everything we have said. What you will remember most is that I love you and will always be there to help guide you through your whole life. Good night and sweet dreams. I'll see you in the morning."

Grandma grabbed a necklace hanging from her neck, grabbed Ms. Daisy's hand, mumbled something and both disappeared.

Chapter 2

Isabel sat on the steps at the interior entry door from the garage and tied the laces of her sneakers. She had hardly slept a wink after her grandma and Ms. Daisy's visit the night before. Even when she woke this morning, she lay quietly in bed mulling over what had taken place. It's not often, a young woman discovers her grandmother is a "Witch".

Perhaps last night was all a dream, she thought but how could she explain Ms. Daisy's witch hat sitting on her bedside table? She even picked it up and inspected it again. Besides, her cheek was still sore where she had pinched herself. She also couldn't explain how she went into Josh's room and found him sleeping with his baseball bat and finding Ethan's ball glove lying on the floor in his room. She would have to think more about the entire episode.

Isabel bent over and picked up her volleyball. She then went outside to the driveway to practice her volleyball serves and return shots.

Bounce, bounce, toss, slap. Darn, too hard, she thought to herself. Even at five foot four, she couldn't reach the ricocheting return off the garage door. The volleyball flew back over her head. She turned to give chase down the driveway before the ball rolled into the street.

Isabel turned quickly not expecting to see anyone and jumped in surprise as Grandmother Wilma stood there holding Isabel's volleyball and smiling at her.

Her Grandma was dressed in her idea of everyday street clothes: a beautiful blue velvet-jogging suit and white Nike walking shoes. Her hair was short and expertly groomed. A very pretty woman by any standard most would say.

Isabel gave off a startled yelp and then said, "Hi, I didn't hear your car drive up. Where's Grandpa? And, where is your car?"

"Now dear there you go again, asking two questions at once. You don't even take a breath", Grandma said and shook her head. "Now. . . question number one; Grandpa is playing golf. Question two; I didn't use my car this time."

"Then how did you get here?" On second thought, I don't want to know."

"Actually . . . that is why I am here. Not only 'how' I got here but 'why' I'm here."

"I didn't sleep more than a wink last night after you and Ms. Daisy left," Isabel said.

"Ms. Daisy and I came to visit because we were in a predicament. I found no alternative but to tell you I was a 'Witch', albeit a "GOOD" witch. Grandma used her fingers as a sign to indicate quotation marks after the word 'good' and to emphasize it.

"While Ms. Daisy and I were here, I discovered you to be far more mature than a normal 16-year-old and far more intelligent too. So . . . I decided it was about time to explain some things about our ancestry. Until now, the code of our craft forbids me from talking to you about it."

"I don't understand. What do you mean by 'It'? There are so many questions I want to ask you."

Grandma cut her off in mid-sentence...

"Let's start by asking one question at a time. I know you're excited, and your mind is running a mile a minute, but we must take our time dear."

"When can we start?"

"Now if you like."

"I'm ready."

Grandma took Isabel's hand with her right and placed the volleyball she was holding between her legs. With her left hand, she grabbed her pretty necklace and said, "Take us from this place we stand to the shade of a tree in a family parkland".

In the blink of an eye, they were in a park and sitting on a bench in a secluded area shaded by several large pin oak trees. Isabel recognized the park as the place her parents took her and her brothers on bike rides.

As they sat, Isabel noticed Grandma was still holding the volleyball between her legs.

Grandma saw Isabel staring at the volleyball. Her face reddened and she put the ball beside them on the park bench.

Isabel decided not to go any further with that thought and instead asked, "Now that's what I'm talking about. How did you do that? A second ago, we were standing on my driveway now we're in the park. Cool."

"That is just the beginning," Grandma said.

"I can't wait," Isabel said. "Where's your black witch's costume?"

"I don't wear my black gown often. It scares people. Ms. Daisy and I were at a 'Sovereign Sisterhood of Good Witches meeting that requires you to be in full craft regalia. I never expected you would catch me dressed up like that."

"I must say I was a little scared at first. I like you better in ordinary clothes, and in daylight," Isabel said.

Grandma smiled. "I think the best way for me to start is from the beginning." Grandma moved her hands smoothing her blue velvet pants.

"Everyone who enters the craft before the legal age of the land must start at the accepted apprentice position. What you're about to embark on will take a long time to accomplish."

"I have the time. What craft"?

Her grandmother ignored the question and said, "Good. It will be like going through school again but the subjects you'll be taking are far more complicated. That's why maturity and intelligence are so important. "

"I'm all ears."

"No dear, your ears are normal for your age and accent your head just the way they should."

"What I meant to say is I'm excited and eager to listen to what you have to say."

"Of course, dear I know that", Grandma smiled. "Now... the witch part of your family goes back many years. Your ancient grandmother received the opportunity to be a 'Good Witch' during the period of transformation when good witches separated themselves from the not-so-good ones. It was a time when the world was full of bad stuff. "

"Was that called the Middle Ages?"

"Roughly in that time frame give or take a few millenniums", she said and continued. "The good witches joined together and created a good witch charter to address the code of ethics and conduct for the sisterhood. Thereafter, each child born into the family of a good witch, and who has reached eighteen years of age, is allowed to join our craft. Some young people, such as yourself, upon reaching a high level of intelligence and maturity before their eighteenth birthday but at least having reached sixteen years of age are given the chance to become an apprentice good witch." She took a big breath after such a long sentence.

"Only one opportunity is provided to start the never-ending learning process of becoming a 'Good Witch'.

"Why me?"

"You are the next in the line of succession dear. I gave your father the chance to be a witch, but he wasn't ready."

"Did you ever ask him again?"

"He only had one chance. He didn't believe me, so I had to let it go. His decision severed his line of succession. When you were born, the opportunity opened again. In other words, you can become a certified and accredited good witch and bridge the 'Line of Succession."

"You said my dad could be a witch, you meant 'Warlock,' right?"

"No, I mean 'Witch'. The word witch has nothing to do with gender. Hollywood uses that word incorrectly in their fantasy films. There are various kinds of witches ranging from 'good' to 'bad'. Centuries ago, people used the word Witch as a term to blame human misfortune on the supernatural. Later on, people divided witches into 'branches. In our family, we decided to join the 'Good Branch.' It's all about the way you think and your interest in helping others."

"Exactly how I feel. I always love helping others."

"With the line of succession severed, it's up to you to mend the break or decide against joining me and your ancestors."

"When do I make my decision? I need some time to get to know what this is all about," Isabel said.

"The only decision you ever make is to say 'Yes' and your training can begin. Or, . . . say no and this meeting has never happened.

Grandma continued, "Should you stop your training at any time, your memory of what you have been taught will be erased and you will continue your life as usual. We are good witches. We have no retaliation practices or punishment. If you decide not to join us or later on decide to leave the order, so be it."

"I would love to be a 'Good Witch'. What do I do to start?"

"Once nominated by a good witch of your family, as an apprentice you must then be accepted by the Sovereign Sisterhood of Good Witches. Upon their acceptance of you, they present you with a special necklace called an 'ANKH': pronounced like the word

'ONK' or 'bonk' without the 'B' sound. You must always wear the Ankh. Without it, you have no powers. "

"Onk," you say. Isabel pointed to a beautiful set of diamond stones peeking through an opening of her grandmother's blue velvet top.

"Is that your Ankh," Isabel asked.

"As a matter of fact, it is."

She withdrew her Ankh from the opening of her top using her fingers as a backdrop for Isabel's closer inspection but without removing it from her neck.

The diamond cluster consisted of a large center stone surrounded by a litter of several smaller ones all encased in an intricately carved gold setting. Even the gold chain that held the Ankh was unlike anything Isabel had ever seen. It appeared to be a tangle of hair-like gold fibers expertly braided into a long rope chain.

"It's very beautiful."

"Thank you, my dear. Diamond is my birthstone."

'The 'Onk' as you say it, is spelled 'A n k h', in case you ever need to write the word. The Ankh is the ancient symbol of life. In our craft, an Ankh is given to each new apprentice."

She took a black velvet ring box from her jacket pocket and handed it to her.

Isabel opened the box to discover a small but the most beautiful golden-colored stone shaped in the style of a heart. She picked it up delicately with her fingers and a shiver went through her body.

"It's your birthstone: Imperial Topaz."

The body of the main stone was a magnificent deep orange with pinkish undertones. Unlike her grandma's Ankh, Isabel's Ankh was corralled by an elaborate gold setting but without the small accent stones like her grandmother's. The same fibrous braided rope chain was threaded through a small loop allowing the chain to hold the stone as a necklace. The sun's rays made the Ankh gleam several colors from inside its setting. It sparkled from dark orange to red to gold then to yellow depending on the intricate angle the sunlight hit its core.

It was much more than a beautiful necklace but the words to describe it wouldn't come to Isabel.

"Is this for me?"

"Yes, my dear. It is your Ankh. Each year on the anniversary of your being accepted into the craft, or for an act of meritorious conduct, a new accent stone is added to the perimeter."

"You must have done a lot of great things to have so many accent stones," Isabel said.

"Perhaps one or two," Grandma said modestly. Her face blushed slightly, and she replied, "But most are annual service stones".

She took Isabel's ankh, placed the gold necklace over Isabel's head, and let it dangle from her neck.

"The Ankh supports our needs of vitality and health. It also points us in the right direction with hope, energy, and love for all people."

"We also add a little something of our own, Grandma said. "A spell you might say."

"You add a spell? What kind of spell?"

"The spell added to the Ankh provides guidance to all the sisterhood. At any time a good witch ventures into the realm of danger, the ANKH begins to vibrate. The vibration is a warning. Your Ankh is also your means of teleportation after you learn to use it."

"Wow", Isabel said. "What's next?"

"The next thing we'll do is choose a 'palindrome', your special code word," Grandma explained. "If you remember, a palindrome is a word spelled the same forward and reverse. Words like the word 'Mom or Dad'. A witch's palindrome, Grandma made the imaginary quote sign with her fingers for the word witches, has to be a little more complex. We use an ordinary word that when spelled in reverse becomes a different word: like 'stop' and in reverse is 'pots' get it?"

"I like 'STOP' and 'POTS,'" Isabel said. "It's easy to remember."

"Okay, here's the deal", Grandma said. She used her fingers again as imaginary quotation marks for the word deal.

"Your palindrome is used in emergencies to protect you or someone else. You are not to use it for a bad purpose, or it will be taken from you. You may even lose it forever and cancel your 'Good Witch' apprenticeship."

"That sounds severe for a simple mistake."

"The gifts you will learn are powerful and can never be underestimated or misused. There are no simple mistakes nor are there second chances when it comes to using your Ankh against another. Even a bad witch. I know that sounds harsh, but that is the law of the Supreme Council."

"I understand. Isabel said and nodded her head in extra confirmation.

"When you use your palindrome, grab the Ankh with your thumb and first finger of your left hand and say 'STOP.' Everything will stop. To bring everything back to where it was, hold your ankh as before but with your right thumb, and finger, and say 'Pots'. Since there are four letters in the word 'stop', you are allowed four minutes to reverse the spell. If you miss the four-minute deadline your next chance will be four hours, then four days, then four months, then four years, then it will last forever."

"Wow, that sounds scary."

"During your apprenticeship, you will have another word, a true palindrome. You pronounce it 'EMPLE-HAM-DNARG' It's a call to me for help and it's

'Grandma help Me' spelled and said backwards. I just made that up." She smiled at her cleverness.

"So, if I get in trouble and need your help, all I say is what," Isabel said and looked confused.

"EMPLE HAM DNARG?" Grandma said.

"How can I ever remember to say something like that?"

"Then just say 'Grandma Help Me'."

"Why do we do all the backwards stuff?"

"All you do is repeat it enough times and you'll remember. If you get in a pinch, call me."

"What if you're on a trip or out of the country somewhere?"

"Whenever you say that phrase, I will come to you instantly no matter where I may be."

"Awesome. . . I feel far more confident. What's next," Isabel asked.

"I think we've done enough for today. You'll need time to digest the things I've told you."

Grandma held Isabel with one hand, touched her ankh with the fingers and thumb of her right hand, and said. "Take us from this peaceful park back to the place from whence we had our start."

In a blink of an eye, they were back standing on the driveway just as if they had never left.

Grandma was now holding Isabel's volleyball between her legs again.

Her grandmother glanced down and noticed the volleyball. She stared quizzically at the ball and held her finger to her chin then she remembered. "I've only got two hands you know." She tossed the ball to Isabel 'hot potato style. She dropped it and bent over to pick it up as it bounced. When she stood her grandma was gone.

It was difficult for Isabel to imagine that this was really happening. She was excited and wanted to try her newfound skills.

Chapter 3

As Isabel walked back up the driveway towards the house, the garage door rolled up to open. Mom had her dog, Snowflake, on a leash.

"Isabel, please take Snowflake for a little potty walk."

She handed her the leash. Snowflake automatically headed for the front lawn, which was her favorite potty spot.

Isabel's mind was reeling with all the possibilities of her newfound knowledge. When Snowflake finished her potty, they went back to the garage. Now she could try something.

Isabel's mom parked her minivan in its usual spot with the doors open. Snowflake yanked the leash from Isabel's hand and jumped into the front seat of the van. She wanted to go 'Bye-Bye'.

Isabel couldn't help herself; she moved her hand and fingers of her left hand to her ankh. She peeked at Snowflake in the van and said her palindrome, "Stop!" Everything stopped just as Grandma had said it would.

There was no sound and Snowflake was resting her paws on the steering wheel standing statue still.

It works. She said aloud and jumped up and down clapping her hands in excitement. She couldn't imagine all the wonderful things she could do now that she had this awesome spell. As she marveled at her handiwork, she heard the back door leading into the house begin to open. She snapped around in panic. She grabbed her ankh with her left thumb and finger, turned to the back door, and said 'STOP!' The door stopped moving. She could only guess that when her mom started to open the door she said "Stop" and everything froze in place.

She turned quickly to her mom's van to reverse the spell and get Snowflake back to normal. In her excitement, she grabbed her ankh with her left thumb and finger, stared at the van, and said the word 'SPOTS' by mistake. She knew she had said the wrong word the second she said it and shook her head in disbelief.

Right before her eyes, her mom's white van was now covered in black spots in a multitude of sizes. It looked like a giant Dalmatian that was terribly deformed. Inside the van poor little Snowflake once a white miniature poodle was also covered in black spots. She posed like a miniature Dalmatian poodle mixed breed of some kind. She looked kinda cute.

She finally came to her senses and realized she had less than four minutes to reverse the spell.

Now... what was it that grandma said about calling her when I was in trouble? She grabbed her ankh, turned to the van, and said" Gree-la-pea. "She stood there waiting for something to happen, it did. Two tires from the van rolled off, came to her, and stopped like two obedient dogs coming when called. The van levitated off the driveway floor without tilting, as you would expect. She used the wrong word again.

What have I done, she said to myself going into hyper-panic mode. Let's stop everything and start over. I must think. The words I'm supposed to say is 'grandma help me' spelled and said in reverse. I can't make any more mistakes. 'Am agree'... no no, 'abledrag, no... I'll get a pencil and write it down she thought.

She ran to the back door of the house that was located off the gazebo deck her dad had made and grabbed the doorknob pushing the door open. Nothing moved. She could see a darkened shadow of her mom frozen behind the door leading into the garage.

She scrambled through the kitchen. Her Mom stood like a statue with her hand extended to the doorknob.

A pencil was lying on the desktop by the back door where the family left messages for each other. Isabel grabbed it and started scribbling on an opened envelope sitting on the desk. First, she wrote 'Grandma help me'. Using what she had printed she wrote the word 'emple-ham-dnarg. 'That's it she said to herself excitedly. 'EMPLE HAM DNARG'. Okay here goes. She rethought what she was about to do. Isabel couldn't make another mistake, so she ran back to the garage to call Grandma in the normal way.

She grabbed her ankh with her right hand and yelled aloud. "Grandma Help Me!"

"What is it dear?" Grandma said.

Startled, Isabel spun around to see her grandma standing beside her in the garage with her hair all frumped up and wearing a white plastic apron thing around her neck.

"At the hairdresser?" Isabel asked.

"Yup," Grandma said.

"I'm so happy to see you. I was trying my new spell and it worked fine. When I went to reverse the spell, Mom came to the door, and I panicked. I said the word 'Spots,' rather than 'pots' as I should have.

"And?" Grandma said looking a little annoyed.

Isabel pointed at the van. You can see it's covered in spots and so is Snowflake. After making two mistakes, I can't reverse the spell on Mom because I don't want her to see her van covered with black spots and Snowflake looking like a miniature Dalmatian. She's standing there now holding the doorknob like a manikin from Dillard's store.

"The tires are looking rather strange sitting in the middle of the floor. Can I presume these are from the van?"

"You can. One thing went wrong right after the other."

"Yes, I can see that."

"What am I going to do?" she asked.

"There's nothing wrong with practicing," Grandma said. She had regained her usual calm and understanding appearance except for the frumped-up hair and white plastic thing around her neck.

"We'll start again from the beginning and reverse everything. It's like we did when Ms. Daisy reversed the spell on Josh and Ethan last night. "

"We don't have much time Grandma."

"Okay, let's try to get the tires back on the van. What did you say?"

"I think I said 'Gree-La Pea?"

"Where in 'shark's teeth' did you come up with that?"

"I was trying to say 'Grandma-help-me'. It came out wrong."

"Okay. . . let's write it down and then, again backward."

Isabel wrote the word 'gree-la-pea' and then reversed it to read, 'aep-ale-erg'.

"AEP-ALE-ERG," she said looking at the tires and holding her ankh. In a flash, the tires moved back in place on the van.

"Yahoo!" she screamed.

"That worked fine," Grandma said. "Let's do the other words."

Isabel wrote down the word "SPOTS" and then in reverse "STOPS".

She held her ankh in her right hand, peeked at the van, and said. "STOPS!" The spots disappeared leaving the van and snowflake as they were before she started playing.

"Good," Grandma said. "Let's get everything back to normal. I don't want to be here when your mom comes from the house. Do you think you can take it from here?"

"You bet", she said and gave her grandma a hug. "Thanks", she said and smiled.

With Grandma still standing beside her, she held her ankh, looked at the door, and said "POTS!"

The door slowly swung open, and Mom stood there. Thank goodness for that, she said to herself and turned to Grandma with a smile only to find her gone.

Snowflake jumped down to the floor of the garage and raced to the back door glancing over her shoulder as she ran past Isabel.

"Did Snowflake do her business," Mom said.

"She had both a number one and a number two."

"Thanks for taking care of that." Mom smiled and closed the door.

Isabel bent over putting her hands on her knees and shook her head back and forth. That was close. I'll have to get a better handle on this before I really mess up.

Her brothers Josh and Ethan rode their bikes up the driveway dropped them on the grass and headed for the trampoline.

If I wanted to try something out, I should have tried it on those two, she thought to herself.

Isabel glanced towards her brothers as they bounced up and down. On second thought, there'll be enough time for that. She smiled to herself, grabbed her volleyball from the garage floor, and dribbled outside for more serving practice.

Chapter 4

Her Grandma drops by every day now. Only for a minute or so, to share a little more of the family history or explain how a new spell works.

She tests her on everything she has taught her. Isabel can see in her grandmother's eyes and facial expressions that she's pleased with her progress.

"Your father decided not to join the good witch branch and I was concerned for his future offspring. I somehow imagined they would all be held back you might say. You seem to have proven me wrong. It appears that you are a natural fast learner."

"I take that as a compliment Grandma."

"More than a compliment my dear, it's a statement of fact. I feel I've stumbled upon someone whose ability will go far beyond a grandmother's teaching skills even with my masters in the subject. You will need a much higher level. You know, kind of like going to university when you are only sixteen."

"Do you think so, Grandma?"

"There's no question about it. That is why I decided to take you with me to 'The Sovereign Sisterhood of Good Witches' apprentice gathering. It will allow you to meet other apprentices. Some you already know."

"I do?"

"Yup. I have also arranged an introductory audience with 'Her Goodness, Sovereign Lady Gwenellen', the Sovereign Sister of Scholars. She is the most educated of our sisterhood and holds the office as our leader, the highest station anyone can achieve."

"That sounds exciting. When do we go?"

"Tonight, at midnight on the dot," Grandma stated.

"Why at midnight all the time."

"At that time of night, most everyone is sleeping. There's less chance of interruption."

"Anytime is fine with me, I haven't been sleeping these last few nights anyhow," Isabel said.

"What do you mean dear?"

"I know I'm probably reacting to my newfound knowledge and overreacting, by having this reoccurring stressful dream."

"Why don't you take a minute and explain your dream to me."

"It's only a dream Grandma: probably from some undigested food like in the novel 'A Christmas Carol.'"

"Tell me anyhow dear."

"I'll try. The dream starts with huge lightning strikes followed by a deafening drum roll of thunder and then a large billow of sparkles like you'd see at fireworks displays. The sparkles funnel from the ground to the clouds rather than bursting in the sky and cascading to the ground like normal fireworks.

Isabel used her arms to illustrate the umbrella effect of the fireworks she was describing.

The next part is like looking through fog or smoke, but I know somehow that I'm at a rock concert and recognize the music. I can see a band playing and the lead singer at the microphone. They slowly come into focus, and I see mean faces painted in black and white. They are witches, old, decrepit, and ugly faces under the makeup. I know it's Lucifer's Lockets because the song they are playing is their hit single. I can't stand to look at their faces they're so evil and wicked, but I recognize each as a member of the rock group."

She glanced up at her grandma. Grandma Wilma sat there with eyes as large as golf balls and her mouth open in disbelief.

"Shall I go on?"

"By all means my dear."

"Flashes of daylight then darkness appear in the background as the band plays its famous hit song 'Give me a minute of your time.' The flashes of daylight and darkness seem to mean the passage of time. Perhaps each flash of daylight means another day and each flash of darkness is another night. I also hear voices, young voices, screaming from the audience."

"Can you hear what they're saying?'

"The song has a refrain that prompts the crowd to rely on singing 'YES' with the band: The band asks, 'Give me a minute of your time.' When their fans answer 'YES', thousands of little sparkles like fireflies, flash over their heads and gather in a cluster. Next, the little lights streak up into the sky and disappear."

"Do go on my dear."

"I'm standing in the audience watching this all happen. A young girl throws herself at my feet and wraps her arms around my legs. She's sobbing. She looks up at me with tears streaming down her cheeks and says, 'Please stop them, they're stealing my life. Please help me, they're stealing my life.' Then I wake up in a state of panic and fear."

"Is there anything else you can remember?"

"Yes, there is and it's the scariest part. I'm looking down at the sobbing young girl, and with each flash of daylight, the young girl appears to be getting older. Others gather around and they seem to grow older as I watch. They beg me for help too. I want to help but I don't know what to do. In my heart, I know someone expects me to do something. It is my responsibility to do something."

Grandma's face is pale from shock. Isabel can tell her grandma's facial expressions are from things that she told her about her dream. She can see in her eyes that she understands more than she was prepared to say.

"I'm glad we're going to the Supreme Council meeting and I'm glad you told me about your dream."

"There's one more thing I remember."

"What would that be?"

"At some point, my attention is drawn to the Golden Lockets each band member wears around their necks. When they started to sing their lockets sparkled like crystal. As the song continues, the lockets gradually turn ruby red a little at a time just like a glass being filled with tomato juice."

"I understand."

"Does the dream mean anything to you, Grandma?"

"More than you can know or could understand. We'll want to discuss this with Gwenellen when we meet."

Chapter 5

At the first stroke of midnight from the old Grandfather clock at their front door, she was looking out her bedroom window hoping to get a glimpse of her grandma on a broom or something. Grandma tapped her on the shoulder. She gasped in surprise and couldn't help but jump from the unexpected touch.

"You scared me."

Grandma was dressed in full witch regalia: pointy hat, neck-to-floor black crushed velvet gown, with the toes of shiny black shoes protruding from under her dress.

"Why should I scare you, I told you to be ready at midnight?"

"I know but everything we're doing is scary to me. I never know what to expect next. By the way, did I ever tell you I have severe motion sickness?"

"You're safe with me," Grandma said and grabbed her hand. "There's no sense of motion when we transport ourselves."

"Good", Isabel said and crushed her eyes closed.

"Take us from this place called home to the meeting place called 'Witch's Dome'," Grandma whispered.

At that exact moment, Isabel could feel herself being lifted and traveling at a fast rate of speed. Her stomach flipped and the remains of her bedtime snack hurled and landed at her feet on a tiled ballroom floor.

When she lifted her head, she heard a murmur of 'yuks' and saw hundreds of people looking at her, then to the floor. She knew what they were "Yuk-ing about."

"Did I mention I had motion sickness," Isabel asked.

"You did my dear and I failed to realize the severity of your condition."

Grandma pointed her pointy stick at the mess on the floor, said a few indiscernible words, and touched her Ankh. The mess disappeared.

Isabel's mouth was open in shock, but she felt better.

"Grandma said another mixture of words to fix the motion sickness problem so Isabel would not have another occurrence on the way home."

All she could think of was to say, "Thank you", and said it.

"Welcome to the 'Witches Dome' the main office of 'The Sovereign Sisterhood of Good Witches' "Grandma said.

Isabel gazed around her. She and Grandma now stood in a grand ballroom with thousands of people on the main floor. The ceilings mirrored the midnight sky with puffy white clouds here and there. A crescent moon was off to one side. The walls also reached towards the sky and huge grooved pillars attached to the walls curved at the top and bent into the ceiling as if holding up a dome.

The sides of the room were hand-carved dark red mahogany wood. At the center of the East wall, a huge, oversized throne-like chair with a red leather back and seat sat prominently displayed. On either side of the throne sat two smaller versions with black leather seating. An aisle covered in red carpet stretched from the throne chair to the edge of the main floor.

"Oh my gosh," Isabel said. "There's a lot of people in full witch's costume but there are also some in ordinary street clothes."

"Those in full regalia, (not a costume) are certified good witches. Those in street clothes are our apprentices who are in varying stages of their training, just like you."

"Oh."

"Welcome again to 'The Sovereign Sisterhood of Good Witches,' headquarters. What do you think?" Grandma asked.

"I have never seen anything like it. It's so beautiful." Isabel said, trying to take everything in as she continued to glance around the room.

"I want you to meet some of the people here. Some you already know."

Grandma put her hand gently on Isabel's back and ushered her towards a group of people on the right. As Isabel approached, two people turned to greet her.

"Welcome apprentice", Aynslee said and smiled.

"Yes welcome", Brianna said and crossed her eyes. Isabel laughed aloud at Brianna's facial expression and the tension she was feeling disappeared.

"Oh my gosh, I didn't know you two were apprentices," Isabel said. "I should have known if one of Grandma's family was an apprenticed witch, I should expect my cousins to be as well."

"Aynslee, the oldest, was the first to be invited as an apprentice. She's been with me for about four years now.

"That's so pretty. "She touched Aynslee's Ankh.

"Both you and Brianna are the same age and are at your first meeting."

"Sounds good," Isabel said.

"I brought Brianna after you, and I talked and had her stay with Aynslee while I went to meet with you."

Isabel gathered her two cousins and hugged them in a sisterly hug. They jumped around in a circle holding hands as they did when they were little kids.

"I'm so excited," Isabel said. "I'm so glad you're here. Not only are we family, but we can help each other as we progress."

"I was hoping you would see it that way," Grandma said.

Three loud thumps silenced the entire room. A witch in full regalia but with gold trim here and there on her black gown stood at the corner of the aisle leading to the throne chair. In her right hand, she held a tall wooden staff with a silver globe on the end.

"As 'Sergeant in Arms,' I command this meeting of 'The Sovereign Sisterhood of Good Witches' come to order. Everyone, please be seated. "

A massive rumble of feet was the only sound as everyone headed to the pew seating on the outside walls. Grandma gathered us in her outstretched arms and herded us to our seats.

With everyone seated, the Sergeant at Arms said, "All rise and recognize our sovereign leader, Her Goodness, Sister Gwenellen."

A tall, slim, and beautiful woman dressed in white satin entered the room to a thunderous standing ovation. Her pointy hat had a gold band. Her pointy stick was gold with silver leaves on the shaft and a brilliant crystal orb at the top. She appeared from the left side of the room and walked gracefully to her place in front of the throne chair. Two other witches of senior status followed her and positioned themselves in front of the smaller throne chairs to the left and right of her "Goodness".

"Please be seated," her Goodness said. Everyone sat quietly: Not a whisper from the mass of people in the room.

"This meeting is more of a friendly get-to-know-each-other gathering. As such I respectfully request our secretary-treasurer to dispense with the formal protocol so we can enjoy our old friends and new apprentices."

"I move to dispense this meeting," the secretary-treasurer said with proper protocol.

"I second that motion," someone said from the other side of the room.

"The motion has been duly made and seconded," said the secretary-treasurer. "All in favor say yea."

The room exploded in a simultaneous yell of "YEA".

"Those opposed, say nay." Not a sound was heard.

"The Yeas' have it. Let it be recorded that this meeting is now adjourned and will be shown in the minutes as 'a grand get acquainted' meeting."

"All rise," the Sergeant at Arms said. "This meeting is now adjourned."

Her Goodness rose from the throne chair and walked down the red-carpeted aisle to the main floor. No one else moved. Her Goodness walked to the main floor, raised her arms, and signaled all to join her. Everyone moved at once.

Chapter 6

The first hour was an obligatory phase of meeting everyone you could meet. Most names were forgotten seconds after being given. Isabel stayed close to her grandma, Aynslee, and Brianna. As they mingled, Isabel noticed from the corner of my eye that caterers started preparing tables in the middle of the grand ballroom floor and loading them with mountains of food.

Isabel is a fussy eater, with absolute likes and dislikes in food. Brianna on the other hand, (who's known in the family to be a ravenous eater,) was mesmerized by the site of all the different delicacies and memorized where her best-loved dishes were located.

"Grandma, I don't think I can meet another person," Brianna said.

"Me either," Aynslee said.

"I know this is tiring," Grandma said. "Perhaps you three could find something to eat while I try to locate Her Goodness Gwenellen and arrange our meeting."

"I hate to do it, but somebody has to help this organization eat all this food," Brianna said. She placed her hands together in an angelic pose and pointed to the heavens in innocence.

Brianna was a tad taller than Isabel and had brown hair and beautiful dark brown eyes. Although she could eat you out of the house and home, she was a fantastic dancer and her daily practice sessions kept her metabolism in overdrive and her waist small.

Aynslee, the oldest cousin, was shorter than Brianna and Isabel, slim, and very attractive. She glanced at Isabel and rolled her eyes upward. They both laughed at Brianna's theatrics and headed with her to the food.

Isabel watched Brianna in horror as she took a chunk of this, a slice of that, and a wedge of something else. Her plate was stacked high with foods Isabel couldn't even imagine having a name. Brianna caught her watching her.

"What?" She said. She slumped her shoulders and turned the palm of her left hand upward.

"What are you going to do with all that food?" Isabel asked.

"You have to try something before you know if you like it or not." She scrunched her shoulders and continued moving to the next platter of exotic morsels.

"There you are," Grandma said. "Her Goodness Gwenellen is waiting for us in the boardroom ". She turned to the cousins, "We'll be right back".

Aynslee smiled and nodded her head at Isabel. She'd been there herself. Brianna continued her treasure hunt down the food line.

Chapter 7

Grandma made three distinct and separate knocks with pauses in between against a huge mahogany door. "Knock. . . Knock. . . Knock. "

"Is this the meeting room?"

"Yes, we call it our boardroom", Grandma said in a whisper.

The door opened without a sound. Grandma guided Isabel in with a hand on her lower back.

Isabel peeked behind the door to see who had opened it but no one was there. What would one expect from a witch get together she thought?

With all the other glorious furnishings she had seen in the Great Hall, this room was a no-nonsense style of deep red mahogany paneling and a full-width bookcase against the farthest wall. A large, long wooden table stretched the length of the room. Plush leather upholstered high-back chairs were spaced uniformly on both sides of a long boardroom table. The woman in the white satin gown was as Isabel suspected, Her Goodness,

Gwenellen. She sat at the head of the table and motioned them forward.

"Come in and sit down", she said and motioned with both arms to either side of the table.

Grandma curtsied politely and Isabel did as well. Isabel had to watch Grandma for directions, as curtsying was not something she was accustomed to. Grandma guided her with another push to her back, and they moved forward to the head of the table. Grandma pulled out a chair on Gwenellen's left side and motioned for her granddaughter to sit down on the right side of the table. She did. Grandma then moved to the other side of the table and sat down as well then shuffled to stand up again.

"Your Goodness..."

Gwenellen cut Grandma off in mid-sentence. "Please call me Gwenellen."

"Thank you," Grandma Wilma said. "Gwenellen, I am proud to introduce you to my second-oldest granddaughter, Isabel."

Gwenellen turned her head towards Isabel and smiled. Grandma motioned with her head for her to stand. Isabel did as requested and with respect to those around her.

"Isabel, how wonderful it is to meet you," Gwenellen said.

"It's wonderful to meet you as well," she said in her most polite and mature manner.

"Contrary to her father's decision not to join us, Isabel is excited about the opportunity. She has been in training with me as her guide and has stumbled upon something I feel you should know about," Grandma said.

"What might that be?"

"Isabel has been having a reoccurring dream of people, young people mostly, begging her for help. Tell Gwenellen your dream dear."

Isabel went into explicit detail about her dream: about the rock concert she had attended in her dream and how the surroundings were bombarded by flashes of daylight and darkness: About the group known as Lucifer's Lockets: How, in her dream, the band members resembled scary Halloween style witches in costume with horrific ugly painted faces. Now this was contrary to the actual real band, she had seen on TV whose members were all young and attractive women even with painted faces.

Isabel told her about the hit song the band had recorded, 'Give Me a Minute of Your Time.' She told her about the sparkles of light like thousands of fireflies that funneled towards the heavens each time the audience said "yes" in response to the song's request of "Give me a minute of your time. "She also explained the strange locket that hung on a gold chain from the neck of the band members and how it changed color from crystal clear to ruby red as they sang. Finally, she explained the cries for help and the wails of grief from the young audience to please help them and how others cried out "They're stealing my life."

Gwenellen was startled as Grandma Wilma had been when Isabel first told her of her dream.

"Please, tell me what's going on. What does all this mean," Isabel asked.

"Remember dear, one question at a time."

"There are many meanings to dreams, and I hesitate trying to analyze what significance yours may have. But... you are not the first to have such a dream", Gwenellen said.

"What does it mean?" Isabel asked insistently.

Gwenellen spoke. "You are aware that many years ago the sisterhood or coven of witches was divided into two chapters. One 'Good' and a... let's say another 'not so good'. We on the good side swore allegiance to our constitution of doing good throughout the world. The other chapter thought our constitution was too confining and chose to make their own rules. The only rule they could agree on as a group, and acceptable to the group of thirteen, was the rule of death. In other words, they could not intentionally 'KILL' another human being. Hundreds of years passed and the thin line between the two chapters has deepened to an unbridgeable chasm. There seems to be little direction or discipline for them so most do as they wish."

"Okay but what does my dream mean," Isabel asked.

"Your dream is an actual rock concert performed by the group called Lucifer's Lockets' as you already know. They perform every night in cities around the world. The images of the band you see on stage are of beautiful young women. They are hundreds of years old. The hit song you refer to has a spell attached. Every time a listener hears the chorus line, 'Give me a minute of your time,' and answers 'yes', a minute is taken away from their lives. The sparkles you see are the minutes being collected and sent to a collection point. No one knows where."

Isabel stood there in shock as Gwenellen explained what was happening.

"The ugly aged faces of the band members you see in your dreams are what they look like without the minutes they steal from their audiences and add later to their own lives."

"How can they be allowed to do that?"

"Originally they searched for those who died unintentionally or were killed in accidents. Before the person died, they asked for the remaining minutes of their lives that was left over before the accident. There was such turmoil over who should have the minutes that the practice was stopped."

"Unbelievable."

"The current practice you witnessed now replaces the old practice and is used in many different ways. The Rock tune idea is the most inventive and introduced hundreds of years ago. It changes with the current trends.

"What about their lockets? They seem to change color from crystal white to ruby red?"

"Their lockets are equivalent to our Ankh", she said and unconsciously touched the charm hanging from a gold chain around her neck.

"They use their lockets the same way we use our Ankh. They also use the lockets as measuring instruments to tell them when they have collected enough minutes to transfer them to a satellite where they collect until downloaded in the same number of minutes to their own lives. The clear color is an empty storage cell and a red locket indicates the cell is full and ready to transfer."

"This is like a science fiction movie. I can't believe this is allowed to happen."

"The group breaks no coven laws so there is not much we can do. They 'ask' permission for a minute of the donor's life and collect the yeses for their personal consumption. We've brought this issue to the Supreme Council and made the decision that technically they did not take a life, so they were allowed to continue."

"There has to be a way to stop them from stealing minutes from unsuspecting people's lives," Isabel said.

"An apprentice does not yet have the training or skills to do anything," Gwenellen said.

"Our charter clearly and specifically states that an apprentice cannot place a spell on any other of the craft be they good or bad and regardless of the deed."

"That is a strict rule of our charter," Grandma said.

"Your Grandma is right. There's nothing you can do."

Grandma stood and nodded her head suggesting she too should stand with her.

"To formally accept you into our sisterhood you must pledge to never hurt another being and work diligently for the betterment of our world," Lady Gwenellen said.

"I promise," Isabel said.

"I acknowledge your pledge in the presence of your Grandmother Wilma and with the power vested in me as the leader of the Sovereign Sisterhood of Good Witches, I accept you into the 'Sisterhood' as an Apprentice Witch."

Lady Gwenellen removed the Ankh Isabel wore and held it lovingly in her right hand.

"This Ankh is a symbol of your devotion to the Sisterhood. Its heart-shaped design goes back to the beginning of our craft. The gem itself is your birthstone, as you know. All Ankhs are clear or better still, 'translucent' to represent the clarity of our mission and the promise you must make to uphold our virtues. The chain of gold setting, which holds your stone, represents the unbroken circle of sisters and the love we have for each other."

She placed the Ankh back on her neck. Isabel had a sudden flush of emotion that nearly brought her to tears.

"Please wear your Ankh as a symbol of your acceptance of the laws of our sisterhood and as a sign of your allegiance to the Sovereign Sisterhood of Good Witches."

"Thank you so much," Isabel said.

The Ankh that hung from its' gold necklace around her neck was so beautiful. Tears finally rolled down her cheeks.

"I thank you as well Lady Gwenellen," Grandma said.

"It was nice to see you again Wilma and wonderful to meet your granddaughter, Isabel. She smiled. "I know our craft will be a little better with you among us Isabel." She lowered her head to read something on the table in front of her, which was the signal to leave.

Grandma made a polite curtsy and Isabel did as well. They turned and left the room.

"What are we going to do now?" Isabel asked when the big door closed behind us.

"We'll discuss it later." Grandma guided me back to Brianna and Aynslee.

"You were confirmed and got your Ankh dedicated by Her Goodness," Aynslee said. "Congratulations." She hugged Isabel hard.

Chapter 8

"Now that you are properly received into the sisterhood," Grandma said," I will teach you our transportation spell that will allow you to return here to use our facilities, especially the library."

"That sounds perfect."

"Okay, now pay attention", she said and smiled.

"When you want to leave an area you must identify it so you know where to return to. At the same time, you must identify where you want to go."

"That sounds rational, "Isabel said.

"Good. When I wanted us to come here, I held my Ankh in my left hand and said the words, 'Take us from this place called home to a meeting place called 'Witches Dome'. In a flash, we were here."

"Sounds easy enough," Isabel said.

"When you want to go home all you do is hold your Ankh with your right hand and say the same phrase but change the location you're coming from and going to."

"Take me from the Witches Dome to a place that I call home."

"Don't forget to say the phrase while you are holding your Ankh in your left hand," Grandma said.

"I'll try it on the way home," Isabel said.

"That will be good practice for you."

"Could we see the library, I'm so excited," she said.

"That will be fine but I have to introduce Brianna to Lady Gwenellen before we do that. Why don't you and Aynslee visit the food line and we'll be right back."

Grandma moved away and spoke to Brianna. They walked towards the boardroom.

Isabel and Aynslee walked the food tables inspecting the contents but tried little.

Grandma and Brianna returned in about fifteen minutes and Brianna wearing her Ankh like the rest of us except hers was Aquamarine, a lovely light blue.

"Congratulations", Isabel said and hugged her. Aynslee did the same.

"Family hug," Brianna said. All four formed a small circle and hugged each other.

"Are we ready for the library?" Isabel asked.

"I don't see why not," Grandma said.

She pointed in the opposite direction from the throne chair. A balcony spread across the entire back wall. Isabel hadn't noticed that end of the building. Ornate wooden rails decorated the front edge of the balcony. She guessed it was to keep someone from falling over the edge. Behind the balcony, a glass wall covered the entire expanse.

"It's up there, Grandma," she said.

They walked to the back of the room where two wide curved staircases wound their way up to the balcony. Dark mahogany panels covered the walls from floor to ceiling with narrow vertical columns concealing where the panels joined. Oil-painted portraits of important women hung in the center of each large panel.

"Who are all these people," Isabel asked. She raised her hand and pointed her finger at one portrait, and then moved her hand in a semicircular path to include all portraits displayed.

"These are important members of our craft who have distinguished themselves above all others in the preservation of peace and happiness in the world," Grandma said." We of the Sisterhood are very proud of our ancestors.

The cousins stopped to view each image they passed and read the brass label riveted to the frame that gave names, dates and titles.

"This old gal could have used a little magic for her face". Brianna quipped. The girls giggled at the comment until Grandma said. "Do not be disrespectful of your elders."

Brianna apologized as did Isabel and Aynslee.

At the top of the stairs, double French doors opened into the library. The smell of stale, musty, old books hit them as they entered. Thousands of books of all shapes and sizes covered the three available walls from floor to ceiling. A rolling ladder attached to a metal bar assisted in reaching the highest volumes.

A lighted ornate podium held a tome that covered its entire flat surface. The huge volume when closed measured at least 8 inches in thickness.

"This is the most revered book in the library," Grandma said.

Isabel walked directly to it and stood as if she were about to make a speech.

The book cover was made of gold and protected the pages inside.

The title read, "The Good Witch Depository of Ancient Spells, Incantations, and Potions", printed in ancient calligraphy.

"The whole enchilada", Brianna added and chuckled. Aynslee and Isabel laughed too. When things got tense Brianna usually had a way to make the girls laugh.

"I guess you could say that", Grandma said with a smile and continued. "Every spell and potion known to the craft is included in this volume. Apprentices are allowed to use this book for research. There's usually a librarian here to help if needed.

"Wow". Isabel swung around using her finger in a semicircular motion again, to indicate the entire room. "What are these books about?"

"These are volumes of the history of the world with the emphasis placed on our craft and the impact we have made. It details all acts of witchcraft before and after the separation of the sisterhood."

"Over there", Aynslee said and pointed to the corner of the library, "is the younger folks' version of the library".

"What do you mean?" Isabel said.

"That is the library's new voice-activated computer center. You ask it a question and it tells you the answer."

"Now that's what I'm talking about," Brianna said. "We would spend years trying to find an answer if I had to use this book."

"True," Grandma said. "But you must have a question and as of yet you're too new to know what to ask."

"I know what you mean," Isabel said. "There are thousands of reference books here. I wouldn't even know where to start."

"I must admit, the computer is a far simpler way to get information than when I was your age. You'll have to make a special username and password to activate the computer. "

Isabel abandoned the idea of using the gold depository book for the simpler computer, which she felt more comfortable with.

"I think it's about time we returned home," Grandma said.

"Do we have to," Isabel said. After she said it, she realized how whiny that sounded and not the mature statement she was trying to make.

"You'll have plenty of time to use the library. We can't do it all in one visit."

"Join hands," Grandma said. She touched her Ankh.

"Take us from the Witches Dome to our separate places we know as home."

The remnants from the snack Isabel ate at the Supreme Council ballroom lay on the magazine she was reading before Grandma came to her bedroom to get her. The blaring green numbers on her bedside clock read midnight then it flashed and read 12:01. In the space of one minute, she had learned a lifetime of new and exciting information. Unfortunately, Grandma's spell to cure her motion sickness problem did not work as she had predicted. Isabel folded the magazine and its contents. She'd throw it in the trash in the morning.

Isabel put on her jammies and jumped into bed. She looked forward to her next visit to the library. Her dream of Lucifer's Lockets continued to bother her. She hoped the library would provide an answer. Tomorrow she would revisit the Witches Dome and start her education.

Chapter 9

Isabel woke early and decided to use the computer at the library to search the internet for information on Lucifer's Lockets. What were their likes and dislikes, living habits and what do they do for fun? She wanted to find out where they lived. A fan would be expected to know these basic facts if they wanted to be considered a real fan. Isabel also wanted to find a flaw that might help in stopping them from stealing minutes from their audience's lives.

Isabel decided to wear her best white shorts and a royal blue top that accented her red hair. She remembered her mom saying, "You're always better off to over-dress than under-dress."

She grabbed her backpack, touched her Ankh, and said, "Take me from this place called home to the 'Ladies Room' at the Witches Dome."

The speedy breakfast she had earlier lay splattered on the tile floor of the restroom. She was now convinced Grandma's spell to stop her motion sickness didn't work. She'd have to ask her grandmother about the incantation she used to clean up her previous spill.

Until then she would have to use a paper towel from the dispenser by the sink to clean up the mess before she headed to the library. After that, she would search for information on Lucifer's Lockets.

"Welcome to our Library", a voice said when she walked through the door.

"Hello. My name is Isabel and I'm a new apprentice doing some research." She sat in the chair provided and glanced around the room but saw no one. "I need to set up a username and password so I can use your computer." She turned to the computer and the reflection of a woman stared back at her.

"My name is Helen and I'm the librarian. Her hand touched Isabel's shoulder and Isabel jumped.

"I didn't mean to startle you," the woman said.

"I'm a bit nervous. This is my first time here," she said to the reflection on the monitor. The reflection moved to her right side and touched her shoulder again.

"You don't have to talk to the monitor, I'm right beside you." Isabel jumped again when she turned her head away from the computer screen and saw the librarian.

"I saw your reflection and thought you were inside the monitor. Like a Genie inside a bottle."

Her face flushed red in embarrassment.

Helen was a tall thin woman with a smile that suggested she was glad I came to the library. She wore a white blouse and black slacks with a black bibbed apron covering her front.

"I'll be more than happy to help you," she said. She moved towards the computer and turned it on.

The computer chimed and the monitor turned on and a female voice said, "Hello, my name is Alice what is your username?

Helen said, "Just say 'New member'".

"New member," she said.

"Great," Alice said. For security reasons, please type in a username you will use when working with me."

She typed "Isabel16."

"Good," Alice said. "Now I need your password. Please type in a password you will use as part of your entry protocol."

Isabel typed 'Snowflake'.

"Thank you," Alice said. "You are now authorized to use this computer. How else can I help you?"

Isabel's excitement level overtook her best-laid plans. "Lucifer's Lockets please." She'd already forgotten the motion sickness spell she planned on researching.

The computer monitors flickered, and then Alice provided pictures on the screen as she described what Isabel was seeing.

The first website under Lucifer Lockets was a picture of Malibu California where they lived. The site provided a roadmap of the area and the names of the Hollywood stars that lived at each address. Most interestingly, the site contained photos of their mansions. For those built more recently an architect's drawing provided the floor plan and gave a glimpse of the simple lifestyle the owners enjoyed. Simple, that was a joke, she thought.

"Lucifer's Lockets home base is shown on page twelve of the local edition of "Homes of the Stars" brochure. The mansion is located in the Malibu oceanfront big-money district. The property is a "basic" fifteen-million-dollar escape consisting of 'two' full acres of groomed lush foliage. A 10-foot-high black wrought iron fence surrounds the property and is electrified to protect the front and sides of the grounds. The oceanfront is open to a deck that provides a scenic view of the beach and ocean. For security, police and private cars pace the boundary streets at irregular intervals. Shall I continue?"

"By all means," Isabel said.

"The architect's drawings shown on the monitor revealed more specific information."

"Could you give me a copy of the interior details?"

"Of course," Alice replied.

The printer booted up somewhere under the countertop.

"There is an attached garage to accommodate guests and personally owned cars. An Olympic-sized pool and tennis courts rounded out the real estate at the ground level outside the mansion.

"The property is barely noticeable from the main roadway. The mansion itself is a circular structure like the hub of a wheel. It has a domed and retractable roof partition, not unlike what you would see at a major observatory. An oversized satellite transponder and receiver replaced a traditional telescope.

Five extensions are running from the circle like the spokes of a wheel. Each extension of the hub is the private and extremely lavish living quarters of one member of the band. Each band member has a staff of five consisting of a live-in chef and four others who care for every aspect of the mansion. The circle or main area of the building contains a large entranceway. Five ornate, red-carpeted winding staircases lead to the entry door of each extension. Off the main entrance is a series of other non-descript rooms from guest bedrooms to several large boardrooms. Beneath the main floor is what is known as the band lab etc. etc. etc."

Alice continued to describe every molecule of the place. Putting her hands in the air Isabel motioned to stop the commentary.

Chapter 10

Isabel called Brianna's cell phone.

"Hi, whatscha doing?"

"Hi, what's up", Brianna said.

"Remember that re-occurring dream I have?" Isabel asked.

"Kind of."

"Well, I'm here at the library and would like another opinion. Could you drop in for a few minutes? I need your help to get this off my mind. "

"Sure. You're at the Witches Dome right?"

"Yes. I'm at the computer in the library."

Isabel turned her back to the monitor and heard the librarian say, "Hello my name is Helen how....

"I'm looking for her," Brianna said.

Isabel turned around and Brianna was pointing her finger at her.

As always, Brianna was dressed casually but like their grandmother, was gorgeous in white pressed shorts and a deep maroon tank top.

Isabel stood and waved Brianna over to the computer. Now she was glad she'd taken her mom's advice and dressed up a little.

"Thanks for coming", she said.

"What's going on?" Brianna asked.

Isabel decided to explain every detail of her dream plus what she learned at the library. For the first time in their relationship as cousins, Brianna was speechless.

"Well?" Isabel said.

"Well, what", Brianna said.

"What are we going to do about it?" Isabel asked.

"What can we do?"

"I don't know, but I feel we should do something."

"Perhaps we could use our new teleportation spell and check things out in Malibu?" Brianna said.

"Malibu…What things?"

"It's obvious we don't know enough to do anything from here. Why don't we go to Malibu and see what we can find out there?" she said.

"Malibu! Are you crazy? I've never been past Denver let alone all the way to California. How would we get our parents' permission to do that?"

Brianna looked at Isabel, crossed her eyes, and said, "Duh! I wasn't planning on asking my parents."

"Just wiggle our noses and GO?" Motion sickness flashed through her mind.

"Yep, you got it, Sherlock." Brianna replied.

"Let me think. . ."

"While you think about it. . ."

Brianna touched her Ankh, grabbed Isabel's hand, and said the magic words. "Take us from the Witches dome to Lucifer's Lockets Malibu home."

Isabel's stomach flipped and she threw up on wet and sandy ground. It was raining hard in Malibu and in seconds, the mess was washed away, and both girls were completely drenched by the rain.

"Should have checked the weather before we left," Isabel said.

"Ya should have gotten some sea-sick pills as well. I thought Grandma cured you of that on witch flights."

"Me to. Guess she used the wrong chant. . . Don't step in that", she said and laughed. Brianna jumped back before she realized the joke.

Chapter 11

Flashes of lightning followed by immediate loud claps of thunder rattled through Malibu. All the lights went out and everything turned grey. Rain smashed heavily on their heads and shoulders. The only dry spots were those under their backpack straps.

"Are you sure we should be doing this?"

"We're here aren't we?" What else do you suggest we do in a rainstorm?"

"Let's pretend we're two inconspicuous tourists taking an after-supper walk along Malibu beach."

"Inconspicuous has left the building. We are now two idiots walking the beach in a thunderstorm," Brianna said.

They walked the beach past the Lockets estate as a precaution, in case someone was there.

"The band is here in California doing a charity thing at Dodger Stadium. I read that in the paper," Isabel said.

"That will help."

They walked slowly past the beach entrance to the Lockets estate.

"I don't see any electric fences," Brianna said.

They probably use some type of motion detector for security," Isabel replied.

The main patio attached to the house had stairs running from the patio deck to the beach. They turned around and walked back.

Their courage increased with the electricity off and no backup lights turned on. They decided to sit on the steps leading from the beach to the house.

"If I saw two people sitting on the beach entrance steps to a large estate and in the pouring rain, I'd call the cops," Isabel said in a whisper.

"Let's give it 15 minutes to allow sufficient time for the police to show up and see if an alarm was triggered," Brianna suggested.

"Okay but let's sit at the deck table with the umbrella and get out of this rain."

After a reasonable length of time waiting in the rain, (say 10 seconds) Brianna's curiosity took over. Isabel was still content to wait 15 minutes at a minimum, but Brianna stood, flipped her rain-drenched hair from her face, and walked to the main door off the deck. She rattled the doorknob.

Isabel stood and waved her hands and arms. "Don't do that."

"Locked," she said in a whisper.

She moved to the right side of the wraparound deck and tried the door there.

"Locked too; what's the matter with these people? Are they expecting someone might try to break into their home in a rainstorm?"

"I can't imagine why they might think that." Isabel put her finger on an improvised dimple on her chin then brushed the rain from her eyebrows. Once again Brianna didn't pay attention to yet another attempt at Isabel's nervous humor. She gave up and rattled the doorknob on the door she was facing.

"Darn, it's unlocked."

Isabel jumped back from the door, as it swung open to the inside as if expecting something to happen perhaps an alarm, a guard dog, or a staff member. She waited for what seemed to be hours but nothing happened.

"Let's get out of this rain."

Chapter 12

Brianna led the way and walked through the door opening. An interior entrance light flashed on.

"They must have backup power somewhere."

They both froze waiting for whatever might happen next. Nothing happened.

"Must be a motion detector light."

"Okay, Sherlock. Are you coming?" She asked. "Or are you going to stand there like a statue with its mouth open and dripping water on the floor?

"This is not something I do every day you know. 'It's better to be cautious than caught."

"And that is our philosophical thought of the moment," Brianna said. She was talking into her hand like a disc jockey talking into a microphone.

Isabel closed the door and locked it. The light went out. She didn't want anyone else to find the door unlocked and come in for a visit while they were still inside.

She slung her backpack around and reached into it for her emergency LED flashlight. Her mom always made her carry it. The map she copied from the internet at the witch's dome was going to come in handy, she thought as she unfolded it.

Isabel stood there dripping wet, trying to orient the map to the actual house floor plan.

"Maybe we should wipe up the water off the floor," Isabel suggested.

"Sure, then we could do the dishes and the laundry."

Isabel ignored her remark.

"Over there", Isabel said and pointed to a door on the right side of the carpeted stairway that led to an upper level. She shone her flashlight at a door for Brianna to see. At the same time, the beam from the flashlight revealed a steel elevator door. On the wall beside the door was a metal cover holding one button with an arrow pointing down.

"Don't even think about using an elevator," Isabel said. "The door chimes in an elevator and the additional lighting could set off an alarm."

They moved to the right of the elevator to another door built into the wall. Brianna tried the knob.

"It's open", she said and smiled back at Isabel with a devilish expression on her face.

"Darn." In her heart, Isabel had hoped someone had locked all the doors when they left. The tour would have ended then and before being caught and sent to jail. She couldn't imagine what her parents would say as she peeked through the bars of a prison cell door.

Brianna pulled the door open and another interior light came on. She started down the stairs. Isabel closed the door and the light went out. Rope lights at the bottom of each step ushered them down. Isabel turned her flashlight off to conserve the batteries.

At the bottom of the stairs, another door blocked their way. Brianna turned the knob to get a sneak peek of the room in case someone was there.

All we need is a little crack to see what is going on but remain unnoticed. More overhead lights flickered and in a second the room was flooded by bright florescent lighting.

Startled, Brianna pulled the door closed and the rope lights came on again.

"Open the door", Isabel said. 'We've already woke everyone up that might be in there."

"Right." She opened the door, and the fluorescent lights flooded a large circular room.

Metal panels containing electronic gauges and meters with illuminated buttons covered the walls. Small lights embedded in the panels twinkled on and off. In the center of the room, was a circle of "Lazy-Boy" type reclining chairs pointing to and surrounding an elaborate computer terminal. The far right panel of the console was noticeably different. Its surface had several small 4-inch diameter monitors each labeled for their specific purpose: Weather, Azimuth, Elevation, and Footprint, plus signal strength meters for the TRIA (Transmit, Receive Integrated Assembly.) She recognized the words from her parents' Direct TV Satellite Dish.

Each panel of the consul had its switching station. Another panel had many controls with labels identifying the outlying circle of chairs. The controls were obviously used to link the control panel to the chairs. The download command switches numbered from one to five and corresponded to numbers painted on the footrest of each chair.

Curiosity took over.

Let's try this mess out," Brianna said. "This is the most sophisticated stereo system I've ever seen. I'll bet the sound is out of this world. "

She flipped the switch to "ON" for panel 3 and chair three. A portion of the wall unit also labeled 3, lighted. The lights blinked on and off like Christmas lights and the internal computer drives began to hum as they booted up.

Brianna jumped into chair 3 and pressed a button on the arm. The back of the chair stopped in the correct position. A helmet appeared over her headrest. She picked it up and fitted it on. The panel to control the satellite gauges and switches turned on automatically.

"Boy are we in trouble now. "She said.

Brianna laughed and gave her a thumbs up.

"This ain't like you. I'm glad to see you joining in the melee."   Brianna laughed again.

"I'm scared out of my mind. I don't know why I let you get me into these crazy things. "

"Okay what do you want to do next?" she asked.

"Go home and pretend this never happened. If we get caught my parents will have a fit not to mention us going to prison for five hundred years. "

"Oh come on, we've come this far, why not ride the whole roller-coaster? If you're going to get in trouble do it right' is my motto. "

A strange mangle of steel pipes formed a cone above the computer terminal. More lights blinked on and off as a signal that told her something was working.

There were far more electronics here than any band would need for their music, she thought.

Mesmerized by the enormity of the blinking lights Isabel moved to the computer panel.

She saw a knob like those on video games that move a player up, down, or from left to right. On the panel monitor, meters with small pointers measured signal strength, elevation, and azimuth. The panel controlled a satellite dish somewhere outside orbiting the earth and corresponded to the gauges inside.

The computer part of the panel was like every other system she had seen. A control keyboard fitted flush with the top of the counter. Another control knob stuck up from the countertop. A circular label gave directions for its use.

On-Pause-Off. Upload and Download were written vertically.

Isabel glanced up from the panel. Brianna was lying on a lazy boy-type chair wearing a headset that resembled a full motorcycle helmet. Her fingers tapped on the armrest of the chair so Isabel suspected she was listening to music.

Isabel decided to join her at a chair closest to the control panel and had a remote keyboard that must be Wi-Fi connected to the computer and satellite display.

She sat down on the chair and heard a buzzing noise. The headset, like what Brianna was wearing appeared from behind her and hovered over her head. She fitted it on and once in place, she rested her head on the back of the chair. Immediately the chair leaned backwards, and she was now lying flat on her back.

She waited to hear something happen from the earphones of her helmet. Instead, she thought she heard the elevator chime. She glanced over at the doors and saw a red arrow shining brightly and pointing up.

She jumped from the chair, yelled "elevator", and pointed towards the elevator doors. In a panic reflex, she pushed the button to upright the chair.

Brianna saw Isabel jump up and point. She glanced at the elevator, saw the red up arrow, and started moving herself.

"I thought you said the band was in concert?" she said, "What are we going to do now?" Humor had left the building and sheer panic replaced it.

"There has to be someplace to hide Dr. Watson," Isabel said in a sarcastic tone of voice. This was not the most humorous moment to use her sarcastic reply to the Sherlock jabs.

Isabel quickly scanned the room. There is only one other door with a knob.

"This way", she said and grabbed Brianna's hand pulling her in the direction she was headed.

The elevator door chimed again to announce its arrival. At the same time, Isabel tried the doorknob. It turned and the door opened to a small broom closet only large enough to fit them inside with the contents that were already there.

She pulled off her backpack and ushered Brianna into the closet. She silently closed the door behind her as the elevator doors opened.

They squashed themselves together into the small closet. There was not enough room to pull the door closed completely so she left it open an inch or so. She was hoping whoever was getting off the elevator was someone other than the cleaning staff who would have to use this room.

"I thought you said they were on tour," Brianna whispered again.

"They are. It must be canceled because of the storm." Isabel said. "Be quiet, and keep your eye open for a chance to escape."

"Sure, as if I was going to fall asleep", she said.

To their shock, the band walked awkwardly through the elevator doors into the room. The fact that all the lights were on didn't seem to register with them.

Their costumes gave them away; otherwise, Isabel would not have recognized them. Each mirrored the image she had in her dream of evil witches, including the wart on the right side of the nose. They walked hunched over and feeble. The skin on their faces resembled cured alligator leather. Their makeup smeared by the rain added to their frightfully grotesque appearance.

Isabel noticed the Ankh on each band member was glowing ruby red.

The band members walked directly to their respective chairs. Without conversation, they settled in their recliner and pushed the button that started the procedure. The chairs reclined and the helmets appeared from their holding box in the back of the chair. Each member fitted the helmets to their heads.

Myra the leader stood at the working console in the middle of the room and was busy pushing buttons. With everyone settled, she pressed a button on the panel for the satellite and everything became active. At the same time, the helmets on each member's head gave off an eerie yellow glow.

"That storm messed up tonight's harvest," Myra said. "I doubt there's enough years to justify a download." A nearly imperceptible grumble came from the other helmets.

Brianna watched over Isabel's shoulder. For the first time that she could remember, she never commented and didn't breathe. Isabel was shaking in terror herself. It was hard to discern who was shaking the most.

Myra rechecked each chair position. Satisfied with all calibrations she watched them blink in sequence in a reverse countdown.

Red, green and orange lights flashed on and off intermittently on the wall panels. The customary hum of the computer hard drives added background noise. Gauge lights flickered as the system came ready to work its magic.

Myra pushed the chair button and waited for her helmet. She fitted it on and glanced at the other chairs once more. Satisfied everything was in order she settled into position, and flipped a switch on the remote keyboard.

The band members lay in their recliners. It was obvious their bodies were changing. The ragged and waning features they had worn minutes ago appeared to be reversing and showed remarkable improvement. Whatever was going on came from the helmets, the satellite console, and a satellite somewhere far above. A blinking red light on the console seemed to be keeping time with the countdown shown on the monitor.

"I think they're in a trance," Isabel said.

"They're sleeping," Brianna said. "Maybe we should bash them on the head, kill the whole group, cut them in pieces, put them in a blender then feed them to the pigs.

"Stop joking around, this may be our only chance to escape."

Isabel opened the closet door a little more so she could get a better view but not wake anyone. Satisfied, she moved out of the closet.

As Brianna pushed herself out, her backpack shoulder strap caught on an old broom that was leaning against the wall in the closet. She lunged forward and grabbed Isabel's shoulders to stop her from falling. Isabel gave her one of her "Are you serious" looks.

She shrugged her shoulders and whispered, "Sorry".

The broom they had disturbed and removed from the closet jumped between them and flew around the room as if looking for a way to escape.

"Couldn't have a witch house without a witch broom could we?"

Each time the broom circled the room they had to duck to avoid being hit. The broom stopped and hovered over the control panel.

"Forget the broom, follow me", she said. "Let's get out here."

Walking on her tiptoes, she moved stealthily to the right of the console and the recliners, just a few steps from the door and freedom. She could feel Brianna wasn't with her. When she turned around, Brianna was standing at the console. She saw Isabel glaring at her and waved at her to come over.

Isabel lip-synced, "Are you crazy?"

She lip-synced back, "Yes I am. Come here quick."

Rolling her eyes never helped and this time was no exception. She moved towards Brianna in her stealthy tiptoe mode gritting her teeth as a sign of displeasure.

"What!" she said, giving her the old 'open hands by her sides' routine: Another piece of body language that she didn't get.

She pointed to a flashing red light on the console. Inside the light lens numbers rolled backwards. "If I read this right, we had 17 seconds before something else will happen," Brianna said. My guess is the download would stop and the folks in the recliners would wake up fully recharged.

Brianna pointed to the download switch.

"So?" Isabel started to move away. Brianna grabbed her shoulder and spun her around. She glanced at the comatose-looking bodies of the band to make sure she hadn't awakened them. All was fine.

Brianna pointed again at the download switch. She pointed at a small circular label Isabel had seen before. "On-Pause-Off" and "Upload - pause - Download".

Isabel's response was the same as before. "So?"

"If we reverse the download to upload, it'll give us more time to get out of here," she whispered.

"Sounds good to me." Isabel's anxiety level was rising out of control.

Brianna pointed at the control knob and said, "You do it."

"Not me Dr. Watson." Isabel shook her head negatively to reinforce that she would not touch the knob.

She gave Isabel a deep sigh and flicked the knob with her finger. It went partway from 'Download' to 'Pause'. "Oops," she said.

Within a second, the band members in the recliners started to rouse.

"Really?" Isabel's eyes enlarged to saucer size from the anxiety she felt.

She took a second glimpse, and sure enough the switch needed to be moved one more position to the right, to "Upload."

The ancient broom made of a tree branch and sticks tied with string, came hovering over the girls. They both ducked in surprise.

The broom hovered over the panel for another second and swished the knob into the upload position. At the same time, the broom drove its shaft down hard on the control knob smashing it into tiny shards of glass. She continued to bash the control panel smashing every dial and gauge. The knobs, lights, and counters were destroyed. Everything was destroyed.

Sparks flew everywhere and the download noise stopped and restarted. She assumed it was in reversing mode and was now starting an upload. As they listened, the hum of the computer raced faster and faster as if trying to escape.

The broom fell to the floor.

"I sure hope it doesn't get mad at us", Brianna said and laughed.

Myra reacted to the switching knob. Her body started to contort and bend unnaturally as she leaned towards the girls.

"You stupid..." she screamed. She couldn't say the words she wanted as she was disappearing as she spoke.

"What did you call us," Brianna asked. You could see she was angry. At the same time, she bent down, picked up the broom, and brought it over her head. It appeared she was going to act out her previous threat to kill the whole group.

"Stop!" Isabel yelled. She held her Ankh in her left hand.

Brianna and everything else froze at her single-word palindrome. "Stop."

Isabel removed the broom from Brianna's hands and leaned it against the computer console. She then grabbed her Ankh and said the word "Pots", which was her reverse palindrome.

Brianna swung down hard with her arms but to no avail, the broom she was going to use as a club was now leaning up against the console.

"Where'd my stick go?" She said

Isabel pointed to the console.

"I think she was going to say, 'Witches', not the 'bad' word," Isabel said.

"Twas a good thing you stepped in when you did Marshall," Brianna said in old west drawl. "I don't take kindly to folks cussin at me much." She continued.

They watched the bodies of the band members, still in their recliners and beginning to wrinkle and wither. All Isabel wanted to do was get out of there. Brianna couldn't pull herself away. They watched Myra and Lucifer's Lockets stiffen and grow old right before our eyes. Their lockets had gone from ruby red to clear crystal.

The upload was reversing their age from young to ancient. Their skin, or what was left of it, reminded her of the mummified remains of the pharaohs seen in an Egyptian history movie. The bodies became so dehydrated they turned to a cloud of brown dust. A haze of white sparkling particles flowed from the recliners to the helmets of the wearers and then into the console. Some sparkling particles escaped from the console air vents and were drawn to the broom that was leaning there.

The volume of the band's bodies deflated. The broom appeared to take form.

They were completely hypnotized by the spectacle. The computers hummed faster and faster and lights flickered at the same rate.

"Should we turn it off?" Brianna said.

"How would you suggest we do that, Dr. Watson?"

"Oh yeah, you're right," Isabel replied when she realized the control panel was pulverized by the broom.

"Would it be too much to ask to leave now?"

Brianna didn't respond.

The hum of the hard drives spinning out of control heightened to a scream as if ready to explode.

Isabel grabbed Brianna by the hand and yanked her towards the stairs. They flew up at lightning speed two risers at a time. They hit the wet deck and slid to a stop.

They peered into the dark sky; more sparkles were collecting outside and formed a chain of light. Within seconds the chain, like a shooting star with a long tail moved upward and towards the east, the direction of the sun and the satellite.

"If I'm not mistaken, that trail of sparkling light is headed to the satellite," Isabel said.

"I'll bet the upload will put the stolen minutes of people's lives back to the right person they were taken from."

"You are absolutely right," a voice said from behind us.

Startled by the voice, they jumped and let out a little scream of surprise.

"Grandma! Are we ever happy to see you!"

"How did you know where to find us?" Brianna asked.

"I got an emergency call for help from an old broom I used to own. "

"How much trouble do you think we're in," Isabel asked.

"In fact, I believe you've done us a great favor. With only a limited amount of knowledge of the craft, you have been able to stop Lucifer's Lockets from stealing minutes from their fan's lives. The upload will go on for hundreds of years just as it was collected. As far as I know, you've not broken any rules and you'll probably receive a 'Goodness" award and stone for your Ankh from the Supreme Council. "

"How about our parents, will they be angry with us?"

"You're with your Grandmother, why would they be angry?" She winked her eye. "Besides I never told them about your apprenticeship."

Grandma took us by the hand and said the magic words. Isabel threw up on her grandmother's shoes as they appeared on Isabel's parents' driveway back home in Kansas City.

"We've got to do something about that throwing-up thing," Grandma said. "It's disgusting."

"I can't help it. Don't step in that," Isabel said.

Brianna immediately looked down and jumped back at the same time.

"Made you look", Isabel said. They all laughed.

The End

www.ingramcontent.com/pod-product-compliance
Lightning Source LLC
LaVergne TN
LVHW051955060526
838201LV00059B/3651